AMELIA MAKES A MOVIE

DAVID MILGRIM

G. P. PUTNAM'S SONS

G. P. PUTNAM'S SONS
A division of Penguin Young Readers Group.
Published by The Penguin Group.
Penguin Group (USA) Inc., 375 Hudson Street, New York, NY 10014, U.S.A.
Penguin Group (Canada), 90 Eglinton Avenue East, Suite 700, Toronto, Ontario M4P 2Y3, Canada
(a division of Pearson Penguin Canada Inc.).
Penguin Books Ltd, 80 Strand, London WC2R 0RL, England.
Penguin Ireland, 25 St. Stephen's Green, Dublin 2, Ireland
(a division of Penguin Books Ltd.).
Penguin Group (Australia), 250 Camberwell Road, Camberwell, Victoria 3124, Australia
(a division of Pearson Australia Group Pty Ltd).
Penguin Books India Pvt Ltd, 11 Community Centre, Panchsheel Park, New Delhi - 110 017, India.
Penguin Group (NZ), 67 Apollo Drive, Rosedale, North Shore 0745, Auckland, New Zealand
(a division of Pearson New Zealand Ltd.).
Penguin Books (South Africa) (Pty) Ltd, 24 Sturdee Avenue, Rosebank, Johannesburg 2196, South Africa.
Penguin Books Ltd, Registered Offices: 80 Strand, London WC2R 0RL, England.

Published simultaneously in Canada.
Manufactured in China by South China Printing Co. Ltd.
Design by Marikka Tamura. Text set in Handwriter Bold.
The art was done in digital ink and digital oil pastel.
Library of Congress Cataloging-in-Publication Data
Milgrim, David. Amelia makes a movie / David Milgrim. p. cm.
Summary: Ably assisted by her younger brother Drew, Amelia makes a home video,
from writing a script and casting herself as the star to hearing
the reviews after their big premiere.
[1. Video recordings—Production and direction—Fiction.
2. Brothers and sisters—Fiction. 3. Stories in rhyme.]
I. Title. PZ8.3.M5776Ame 2008 [E]—dc22 2007018389 ISBN 978-0-399-24670-8
1 3 5 7 9 10 8 6 4 2

For Axel, Annie,
Elliot, and Camila

Mom is on a cleaning spree.

Dad is busy as a bee.

What's to do?
Hey, wait, I know!
Let's make ourselves a video!

A script's the first thing
that we'll need.

We'll choose a cast. I'll play the lead.

You assist, and I'll direct.

I'll need a chair and
full respect.

We'll borrow tools and build a set.

There are scenes to paint and props to get.

Make the costumes,

Feed the crew,

Fix the lights,

And makeup too.

Learn the lines, rehearse, and then rehearse some more, then once again.

Here we go, rehearsal's done,
roll the camera, take scene one!

. . . and . . . ACTION!

Let's take five, discuss the end,
rewrite the script, and shoot again.

. . . and . . . . ACTION!

That's a wrap!
The filming's through.
Hugs and kisses
for the crew.

Record the soundtrack,

Edit the scenes.

Our movie's ready for the screen!

Everyone in town is here.
Get ready for our
big premiere!

Pour the soda,
pop some corn,
watch some hip new
stars be born.

Reviews are in,
the film's a hit!
We've reached the big time,
this is it!

Thank you, thank you,
cast and crew,
and, most of all,
my brother Drew.
I share these cheers
with all of you!

GLOSSARY OF SOME MOVIE-MAKING TERMS

"ACTION": The director's instruction to the actors to begin.

CAST: The actors.

CREW: Everyone involved in making a movie, except the cast.
    This includes the cameraperson, lighting people, sound people,
    makeup artists and others.

"CUT": The director's instruction to everyone to stop.

DIRECTOR: The person who tells everyone what to do.

"EDIT THE SCENES": Choose the best camera shots and put them in order.

"A HIT": Popular.

LEAD: The main actor.

PREMIERE: The first time a movie is shown.

PROPS: Things used in a movie, such as a magic wand or crown.

REVIEW: An opinion of the movie, often published in a newspaper.

"ROLL THE CAMERA": The director's instruction to start filming.

SCRIPT: The written words that actors say in a movie.

SET: The place where a movie is filmed. Often a set is built to look
    like some other place, such as an enchanted forest.

SHOOT: To film.

SOUNDTRACK: The music used in a movie.

STARS: Famous actors.

"TAKE FIVE": Take a five-minute break.

"A WRAP": The end of all filming.